THE
WORLD BEYOND
THE WAVES

AN ENVIRONMENTAL ADVENTURE

What people are saying about:

THE WORLD BEYOND THE WAVES

"A sort of Free Willy *with soul. It takes youngsters into the world of another consciousness. Tenderly, vividly. A journey into the heart of light."*

Bob Hunter
Co-founder of **GREENPEACE**
Winner of Canadian Governor General's award for nonfiction

*"**The World Beyond the Waves** is a truly wonderful book; it embraces all the elements a child can relate to, yet tells the child under no uncertain terms that the earth is a life form which cannot be possessed. Rather, it is a thinking, moving, and feeling entity whose elements must work in synchronicity if life is to flourish. One person can make a difference. If we arrogantly cling to the idea that we are the superior life forms, then we must act as leaders and not followers, and learn from creatures who are not building better bombs or bulldozing precious land—in other words, we must learn from the life forms who are truly superior."*

Cara Sands
President, **FRIENDS OF THE DOLPHINS** (a nonprofit organization with the focus to "re-educate" the public on the plight of dolphins and whales, especially captive cetaceans)

"The rapid disappearance of plant and animal species throughout the world should lead every concerned person to action. This human-centered wave of decimation can be turned around. Education will be a major part of this effort. This book leads us in that direction—towards a kinder, safer, cleaner world."

Rob Laidlaw
Director, **ZOOCHECK CANADA** (a national, registered Canadian animal protection/environmental education charity)

"Much of the work of the International Wildlife Coalition involves trying to gain effective protection for the world's much beleaguered marine animals. Therefore it was inspiring to read Kate Kempton's **The World Beyond the Waves***. May the children who read her book learn from Sam and like her, become kindred spirits and guardians of all the creatures of the oceans. We are proud to endorse this wonderful story."*

Anne Doncaster
Program Director, INTERNATIONAL WILDLIFE COALITION CANADA

"If our world is to survive to the end of the 21st century, the biological education of our children is imperative. It is high time to stop incorporating biology within a fractured "science" curriculum and to instead revert to Natural History, the teaching of which should start in grade one and continue expanding to the end of high school. We must teach live nature and not dead science! In this connection, **The World Beyond the Waves** *offers an important first step towards the education of the young—or of the old, for that matter, for I too have enjoyed it!"*

R.D. Lawrence
Author, IN PRAISE OF WOLVES, CANADA'S NATIONAL PARKS, THE WHITE PUMA and THE NATURAL HISTORY OF CANADA.

*"***The World Beyond the Waves** *is a genuine means of empowering children and thereby facilitating the development of self-esteem. It teaches how the self grows even greater by a broader identification with other living beings for whom we can show empathy and compassion in this great circle of life."*

Dr. Lorin Lindner, Ph.D.
Clinical psychologist and president, FUND FOR WILD NATURE and PSYCHOLOGISTS FOR THE ETHICAL TREATMENT OF ANIMALS.

THE
WORLD BEYOND
THE WAVES

AN ENVIRONMENTAL ADVENTURE

WRITTEN BY KATE KEMPTON
Concept by Carol Trehearn

ILLUSTRATED BY LARRY SALK

Published by
PORTUNUS PUBLISHING CO. ©
3435 Ocean Park Blvd. Suite 203
Santa Monica, CA 90405

Copyright 1995 by Portunus Publishing©
Artwork copyright by Larry Salk.
Text copyright by
Kate Kempton and Carol Trehearn.
All rights reserved.
Printed in Hong Kong.

Design: EGRET DESIGN

Publisher's Cataloging in Publication
(Prepared by Quality Books Inc.)
The World Beyond the Waves
ISBN 0-9641330-1-6
1. Ocean--Juvenile fiction. 2. Marine pollution--
Juvenile fiction. 3. Ocean--Fiction. I. Title.
PS3561.E411W67 1995   813'.54
                                QB194-1572

This book is printed on recycled paper using soy ink.

This book is dedicated to all the animals of the sea
and their fight for survival.

The World Beyond the Waves is endorsed by
CONSERVATION INTERNATIONAL and ZOOCHECK CANADA.

Conservation International is dedicated to the protection of natural
ecosystems and the species that rely on these habitats for survival.

You may contact them at:

1015 18th Street N.W., Suite 1000
Washington D.C. 20036
PHONE: 202 429 5660
FAX: 202 887 5188

174 Spadina Avenue, Suite 508
Toronto, Ontario M5T 2C2
PHONE: 416 366 6100
FAX: 416 360 4383

Zoocheck Canada is a national, registered charity established to protect
wild animals and their natural habitats and wild animals held captive.

You may contact them at:

5334 Yonge Street, Suite 1830
Toronto, Ontario, Canada
M2N 6M2
PHONE / FAX: 416 696 0241

TABLE OF CONTENTS

CHAPTER ONE

THROUGH SAM'S EYES

"REMEMBER WHAT I told you. When the storm hits, do what I say and do it quickly." Uncle Dan put his hand on his niece's shoulder and squeezed. Catching the concern in her eyes, he added, "Don't be frightened. It may not be too bad."

Sam nodded and turned her gaze back to the porthole. The sea was thick as molasses that day; and like molasses, it clung with sticky fingers where it fell. From the glare of the porthole glass, Sam stared at the reflection of her 12-year-old face. Concern still shadowed her features, but the approaching storm was the last thing on her mind. She rubbed her fists over her lids.

She had her father's eyes—big and brown and sloping downward somewhat, like those of a basset hound. Puppy dog eyes. Her mouth was wide and strong and when she smiled, two fat dimples the size of nickels carved hollows in her cheeks. When she was little, her father had rubbed his thumbs in those hollows as if to plug them up. Then he would laugh his deep, loud laugh and say, "Those holes would get filled with lint if I didn't clean them out once in a while." Sam brought her own thumbs to her face now and ran them down the round, soft outline of her cheeks. She liked her face. It was the straight mop of thick brown hair she didn't like. This she got from her mother's side of the family. They were all hardy, healthy people who wore their hair like helmets, warding off the weather. It had suited her mother, framing her beautiful face, with those startling grey-green eyes. Sam would always remember that face, that hair. And she would always remember her father's thumbs. Her mom and dad died in a car accident less than a year ago.

Sam's new family, her aunt and uncle, loved her very much. Sam knew that. But it was hard, so hard, to be 12 and be brave. Sam walked up the stairs to the deck and sat down in the cockpit, bracing herself against the motion of the sailboat as it pounded through the heavy seas. The day had awakened stretching itself through an eerie pink haze. Red sky at morning, sailor take warning . . .

She stared at the swells as they grew fatter and heavier with each roll of the boat. Her expression was more clouded than the weather. "Please, dear, quit moping. You'll frighten the fish," Aunt Margaret said, smiling softly. "I'm fine." Sam was trying to be fine. She had to find some answers that made sense because *nothing* seemed to make sense any more.

On a Saturday ten months ago, her mother had told her that answers come when you least expect them. All you have to do is look for them. "I know you don't understand now," her mother had said, "but we have to go away for a month and someday you'll appreciate why. We have a business to run. And the money we earn lets us buy all the things you want. Please don't be angry."

Sam hadn't really been angry her parents were going away. She had just wanted to go with them. They were leaving for Florida to set up a new office. Sam's mother and father were real estate lawyers in Detroit but they helped a lot of people buy and sell land and houses down south. The next day her grandparents had arrived to look after Sam and her parents had driven away, waving from the car window all the way down the street. That was Sunday. By Monday, her parents were dead. Car accident, she was told. That was the day the world stopped making sense.

Sam lurched forwards as the boat slid down between two big waves. The sea was changing rapidly but there was nothing she could do. Sam and her aunt and uncle had been at sea for more than three weeks. There were no planes, cars, kids, or TV. Sam knew it was wrong, but she almost wished a storm would come because that, at least, would be exciting. There was too much time to think at sea. Think and nothing else. It was big out here. She missed the things that made her feel safe and comfortable and warm. Things like her mom's bedroom. It was big but it never felt empty. Dozens of pictures crowded the walls and dresser tops. Photos of Sam's first birthday. Her second, third—in fact, every birthday. Pictures of Sam on Santa's lap when she was too young to wonder how this hairy, red man could be in so many malls at the same time. A photo of her ice cream-covered face as she sat in bed recuperating from tonsil surgery. And a very large, framed picture of her first day at kindergarten, tears soaking the collar of her new blue dress and her mother's tears clouding the focus.

She missed her own room too, stocked with things she'd long ago forgotten she'd ever wanted. Things bought as much with her parent's love as their money. She was an only child and she had been given enough gadgets and clothes and toys for ten brothers and sisters.

Brothers and sisters she would never have now. Her parents were gone and Sam had been sent to live with her aunt and uncle. She remembered the day she arrived in Boston to meet them. She knew they were researchers, teaching university courses during the school year, then working off their boat in the summer. They met her at the airport and took her to their small, wooden frame house in Cole Harbor. Nothing like her parent's house. There were books and papers everywhere. It looked as if they'd tried to tidy the place up, but their efforts only drew more attention to the mess. They showed her to "her room." It, at least, was neat and organized, except for the mound of stuffed animals thrown all over the bed.

"What are these?" Sam had asked.

"We got them from friends," her aunt had laughed, embarrassed, "but I guess you're too old for them."

Sam looked over at her aunt and uncle steering and working the yacht. They were sailing down to South America and back, doing marine biology research on the way. Aunt Margaret was talking a mile a minute to Uncle Dan. Margaret's voice matched her face. Both were full and round. And when she got excited, her eyebrows danced a jolly jig on her forehead. Sam was fascinated by this sight. Margaret raised her hands as she spoke and her small, plump fingers made circles through the air.

Uncle Dan just sat there and listened patiently. His calmness matched Margaret's passion. He was a big man, stocky. But there were no hard edges. Everything about him was quiet and gentle strength. His head and hands and feet were huge. Deep wrinkles and a full mouth broke up the expanse of his face. Uncle Dan always told the truth. But even when he was forced to say something that might hurt, as truth sometimes did, his kindness softened most of the pain.

Sam liked her aunt and uncle both, but she couldn't quite think of them as her new parents. She wanted desperately to belong to someone. She wanted her mother and father. She wanted friends. She wanted her old life back!

CHAPTER TWO

THE STORM

A CRY OF SUCH pain pierced the air, Sam snapped out of her daydream. She peered over the edge of the boat. Three **bottlenose dolphins*** were circling frantically in the wake. The largest one was bleeding from his side and raising his nose with great effort toward Sam. She felt he was trying to speak. His eyes were wide and filled with torment. He thrashed about until he became so exhausted he could only float helplessly on the surface.

"Help him, please, can we help him?" Sam cried. She leaned over the side and tried to touch the dolphin's smooth, grey body, but he was too far below. The injured animal struggled to push his nose higher, but they could not seem to reach each other. Sam didn't know why, but she understood his pain. And she was determined to make it stop.

Margaret and Dan threw a little rubber dinghy into the sea. The waves were pounding furiously and Dan almost missed the small boat when he lowered himself overboard. He fought the water coming at him from every direction. Sam watched, anxious and afraid, as the dinghy threatened to tip. The dolphin was so hurt and tired, he was barely making a sound now. Only tiny whistles and whimpers escaped him. He kept looking at Sam and Sam, defiant against the force of the approaching storm, kept looking back. She sensed an intense connection and need to protect this creature—he seemed so innocent.

*Words in bold type are discussed in the Glossary. (see page 84)

Dan finally managed to get the raft over to the animal, who did not object to this approach. He seemed to know these people were his friends. Dan examined him as quickly as he could but the sea made everything difficult now.

"Margaret, get me the antibiotic and the syringe," Uncle Dan shouted.

"What's wrong with him?" Sam was afraid she wouldn't like the answer.

"He's been cut by something. I don't know what, but it looks like something man-made. A knife or a net. I'm going to give him a shot of medicine to stop the infection. He's hurt pretty bad."

"Is he going to live? Make him live."

"I'll do what I can. But this storm..."

Dan gave the dolphin the antibiotic. Margaret threw a rope ladder over the side of the sailboat and Dan climbed up to the deck, pulling the rubber dinghy behind him. The dolphin seemed frightened by all this activity but he remained still and stayed close by. Sam knelt near the edge, held onto the lifeline, and kept her watch over the animal. They did not take their eyes off each other. The two other dolphins swam close by and they too, kept up their watch. Why was this creature so special to Sam? She wanted to keep him with her forever.

Just then, a white **tropic bird**, wearing the black mask of a bandit, tried to land on the sails. Long yellow tail streamers guided him expertly through the wind, but the sails kept shifting, fighting him off. The bird, now annoyed, squawked in protest. He finally gave up his attempts to land on the sails, touching down instead on the lifeline next to Sam. He puffed his chest feathers and screeched, poking his funny orange beak toward the dolphins. His little black eyes darted this way and that. Then as quickly as he had come, he left, lifting off on a gust of wind. He circled over the boat once, then flew away.

What had he wanted? What had he said? Sam did not know, but the dolphins seemed to understand. They began to screech too. What was going on? But all her questions were swept away as a wave lurched the boat to its side. Sam's grip tightened on the lifeline.

"Sam, Margaret." There was a sharp edge of concern to Uncle Dan's command. He pointed a thick finger at the horizon. "It's moving fast."

Until now, the weather had been gentle and kind during their voyage. The closest land, the southeastern U.S. coast, was hundreds of miles away. Here, in the middle of nowhere, something very scary had arrived.

Clouds tumbled over the sea, blanketing the distance. The sky seemed to be closing in on the boat, squalls marching like an army with deadly aim. The pink of the morning had shadowed into shades of grey. A low roll of thunder echoed off the Atlantic. Sam looked down. The ocean hollowed beneath her, swelled, then hollowed again. The 50-foot yacht had looked so solid and big in the Boston dock, but it now seemed small. The giant sea tossed it about as if it were a cork.

Sam searched the water for her injured friend. She caught sight of him briefly, and heard his voice as he let out a cry. But a second later the sea swept over all three dolphins and they disappeared in the raging waves. Feeling she had somehow abandoned them, Sam strained to find them again. They were gone.

The light was gone too. The sky was a dark dangerous mass, dropping like a curtain on the boat as if Sam were trapped on a stage, playing out a scene of horror someone else had written. Someone or something else. It wasn't real. The ocean was green-black, but for the white teeth of the waves threatening to bite. A strange and terrifying rhythm took over Sam's world. The ocean opened, then closed. The boat was sucked deeper into the troughs, then flung with teetering madness onto the crests of the waves.

"Get below, Sam," her uncle ordered. "Secure the hatch. And stay there!" Uncle Dan was an experienced sailor, and his experience gave him great respect for the power of the sea. Sam was witnessing this power for the first time. Another rumble of thunder.

"Sam, now!"

An icy slip of fear tickled Sam's spine. The wind prodded at her back as she shivered violently in her jacket and jeans. She took one last look at Uncle Dan fighting the wheel, scrambled below, and slammed the hatch shut above her. The wind whined and scratched at the door. The air smelled of a foul beast, licking at the boat, breathing an odor of salty decay. It was cold, thick, and wet.

Every sound became loud. Every silence became louder. A gale at 50 miles an hour is an uncaring, unstoppable force.

Sam fastened her life vest and clung to her bunk. Through the portholes, she stared at the ocean. The ocean stared back. It was a living thing. A living, growing thing. It yawned wide, then rushed at the windows—at her. Only the narrow glass and walls kept it from pouring inside. Could they keep out the predator much longer? The waves punched the boat down, throwing Sam against the far wall. Books and pillows and pots flew through the room and crashed atop Sam's head.

Sam huddled in the corner. She heard her aunt and uncle working, pulling down sails before the wind chewed them to shreds, shouting over the din. She felt she could hear the pounding of their hearts. But it was her own, hammering against her chest. No, she said. No, she must not panic. She must not cry. Tears streamed down her face.

Huge, bulbous swells rose out of the depths, edges frayed by fierce wind. Sam pressed harder against the wall, then hurtled sideways from the impact of yet another fisted wave. The little boat shook itself, lurched upright, then slammed into the next wave. Over and over and over. Minutes dragged as time itself seemed to be drowning in the vicious sea.

Sam's head throbbed with pain and blood trickled down the right side of her forehead. "Stop!" Sam screamed. No one could hear. She could not hear herself, her voice lost in the boom of the storm.

"Please stop," she whimpered. To her amazement, it did. The rain, the howling wind, it all just stopped. All but the relentless pounding of the waves, smashing against the portholes, trying to get in. Sam had to get out, get away. Her uncle's command to stay below was lost on the waves of Sam's fear. She was more alone now than she had ever been.

She lunged for the latch, fumbled, tore open the hatch and froze. Sam stood, exposed, directly under the eye of the storm, deceived by the eerie stillness. The eye of any storm plays tricks on those trapped inside, mocking them with a sense of false calm. It fooled Sam into thinking the rage had ended. It had not. The worst was yet to come. She had one foot over the washboard when the eye closed, the calm broke. In one shattering second the sky fell in on Sam as a massive crack of thunder splintered the air. The instant before Sam realized her mistake, she caught one glimpse of her aunt and uncle, strapped by safety harnesses to the boat. She never heard their cry of warning, as it was drowned by the sound of menacing force rising up behind her. A sound she would never forget—the hissing of a giant wave. She turned and stared directly into the face of terror itself—a green wall, towering out of the depths. The last thing Sam saw before the wave swept over her was a flash of orange beak and yellow tail.

Then the ocean opened its gaping mouth and swallowed everything in its path.

Sam was pushed down, spinning through the mass of bubbling water. The sea opened into a whirlpool, funnelling her into the depths, forcing her further and further below the surface. Blurred and busy images twisted around her. She was hurled upside down, sideways. Her legs and arms flew out in every direction. Heavy green water surrounded her, tugged at her, swept her, spun her deeper and deeper. How long had she been under? Seconds? Minutes? Sam would never know. She couldn't think. She couldn't breathe. Suddenly, with one loud THUD, the spinning stopped. Sam felt a jolt of pain rip through her entire body. Then everything went black.

CHAPTER THREE

DAPPER
AND THE DREAM

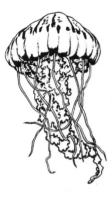

THE AIR WAS cool and, Sam sniffed, very, very clean. She opened her eyes slowly, fluttering. It wasn't dark, but it wasn't quite light either. Sam peered groggily this way and that. Smooth walls surrounded her. There were no corners, no seams. A hollow plinking sound, as regular as a clock, counted off time somewhere beyond her sight. She blinked, tried to focus. Sam knew she should be afraid, and she felt the first little prickles of fear. Yet the peacefulness of the place was like a warm, thick blanket surrounding her, and the fear was smothered before it could rise.

She struggled onto her elbows. But her head began to pound and she fell back again. Sam reached back and explored her scalp. The blood had dried but the bump still throbbed.

I am sick, Sam thought. I am sick and hurt and in a hospital somewhere. She inhaled deeply of the moist air, searching its scent for answers. An uneasy comfort took hold, for despite all, she was alive, she had been found. And she was no longer trapped in the angry sea.

"Yes, you are hurt. And you are in a hospital somewhere." The voice from behind exploded in Sam's ears and real fear, this time, gripped her like metal clamps from which there was no escape. Where am I? Who are you? A dozen questions raced through her mind but none made it to her lips.

"So many questions," said the voice.

Am I talking out loud? Sam stared with huge eyes but the shadows held whoever, whatever, had spoken, from her view. She dared not move. Images of slippery creatures, slithering toward her, nibbled at her mind. The thing in the shadows clicked and scratched. Sam pressed tightly against the floor, willing it to swallow her up. The thing took a couple of steps, but Sam knew not which way. Space and direction seemed lost here.

There was something familiar about the thing, the sounds it made, the way it walked. Sam strained to figure it out, but the answers teased her beyond her grasp. What was it?

"Well, do you want to know who I am?"

"Yes. Well, no, I'm not sure." Sam found her voice. What was it that was so familiar?

"Let me know when you're ready. I'll come back."

"Wait."

But the thing had vanished beyond the walls, catching a flicker of the not-quite-light as it moved. A flash of yellow, that jaunty step, she had seen them somewhere before.

Sam began to cry. What if the thing were some ugly monster from the world of her nightmares, covered in warts and pulsating eyes?

"Ugly? You think I'm ugly? The nerve!" said the voice, this time from over her head. Sam's eyes jolted wide. I know you, I know you.

"In fact," the voice continued, "I'm considered rather a dandy. A dapper young dandy," it preened. Before Sam could blurt out any questions, the creature landed with a rustle just inches away and peered into her startled face.

"Well, don't you agree? Am I not pretty?" Relief and confusion flooded at once through Sam, as a cocky tropic bird strutted beside her. It was the same tropic bird she had seen on the boat.

"You . . . you," Sam stuttered. "You can talk."

"I think, rather," said the tropic bird, "you can understand."

"What's your name?" asked Sam.

"Why, Dapper, of course. I am Dapper the tropic bird. And you are Sam, Sam the Homo sapien."

"How do you know my name?" But Dapper was busy plucking at his white feathers, swishing his yellow tail this way and that as if Sam were but his audience.

"I said, how do you know my name? How do you know what I'm thinking?"

"We animals hear and see many things you humans can't."

Sam figured this was a dream and saw no harm in playing along.

"Where am I? Where are my aunt and uncle? Are they all right?" Sam tried not to let the urgency show in her voice.

"As to the last question, the answer is yes. They are still on their boat. As to the first question, you'll find out soon enough."

"But..."

"Now, try to raise your head a bit and I'll put a pillow of feathers underneath. You're hurt. And asking so many questions will only make your head hurt more." Sam *was* very, very tired. And her brain *was* very, very fuzzy. Slowly, carefully, Sam raised her head. Dapper clucked once then stepped behind her. "Now lie back," he commanded.

"You? You're my pillow?"

"You'll never have a better one. Or a finer looking one. Now sleep."

Sam laid her head against the warm cushion of feathers that was her new-found friend. She could hear the peaceful, steady beat of his heart and it began to lull her to sleep. Sam struggled a bit against the fogginess, but Dapper kept his little body very still. He must have been uncomfortable but Sam soon became too tired to ask. Besides, Sam knew this was all a dream and when she awoke everything would be back to normal and this peculiar world would be where it belonged—in her imagination.

"The things they make me do..." Dapper muttered.

"They?" The rest of Sam's thoughts were lost as she finally gave in to exhaustion.

Her sleep was good, heavy, for a long time. But images began to peer at her from inside her head. Images she could not stop. They were tied together by the magical thread of dreams, a thread that always seemed to break when she awoke, but was so strong here. Her mother came to her then. A round face looking down at Sam as she would a baby. Her eyes were kind and filled with a sparkle of special love. She hummed a song Sam didn't know. Then she was gone, swept away on her music. It wasn't sad, it was just as it was. Sam could still hear the music and now the words drifted toward her. "Don't cry for me. I float above the sea. Don't look for me there. I am everywhere." The song played again. Her father appeared, playing a clarinet. He never played the clarinet. But this dream, as dreams often do, had a life of its own. Her father played louder and louder. Sam wanted him to stop. Please stop. The clarinet flew from her father's grasp and splintered into a thousand pieces. No, cried Sam. I'm sorry. But her father was gone. The music was gone.

She was racing now, in a car—no, a big boat—on the water close to shore. Past houses, streets, factories, offices, garbage cans, signs. Sam tried to jump from the boat, to reach out and grab the city on the shore. But she couldn't move. She strained harder against the will of her dream. But still, she couldn't move. The city was gone and Sam was alone. Why didn't she feel alone? The wind caressed her face, tickled her nose, played with her dark, straight hair. Water splashes kissed her cheek. The whisper of the wind and the patter of the water drops created a melody of sound. 'Don't cry for me. I am the sea.' Sam felt crowded. Nothing was there. Nothing but the air and the water. Light played off the waves, flicking on and off, like a million eyes opening and closing. Eyes and faces that floated up and washed away. Eyes and faces. Peering at her. Stop staring at me.

"Stop staring!" Sam opened her eyes and found herself looking square into the ugliest old face she had ever seen.

CHAPTER FOUR

JACOB'S STORY

EVERYTHING WAS QUIET. The light was somehow brighter, different. It had a greenish glow like that from her aunt and uncle's shipboard computers. That's it! I'm in our boat. Sam shook her head, trying to wake up. "Ow, you're ruffling my feathers." Her pillow shuffled a bit.

Oh no, oh no, oh no. Why can't I wake up? Sam's breath was shallow and sharp. She felt a rising sense of fear and willed the dream to vanish.

But those eyes kept staring at her and when a gurgling noise rose from the crooked mouth beneath, Sam screamed. She was totally and completely awake.

"Who are you?" the creature asked, its hushed and raspy breath echoing off the tomb-like cavern, filling the air with ancient smells of musty museums, of death itself.

"Her name is Sam the Homo sapien," Dapper said.

"I know that. I mean WHO ARE YOU? What is your purpose in life? What were you doing above our world?"

His voice was gravelly, pebbled with age and knowledge, just as her grandfather's was. He rolled his *r*'s and rounded his vowels, creating that gurgling effect.

"My purpose?" Sam asked.

"Your role. Your job."

"I don't have a job. I'm only twelve."

"What do your elders do then?"

"They sail," Dapper chimed in. "They sail a big boat. I saw them. I played on their sails. I . . ."

"Hush, you silly animal. You tropic birds and your friends, the stormy **petrels**—all you seem to do is play. Sit up," he ordered Sam.

Sam sat up, her head still pounding. For the first time, she got a good look at the creature with all the questions. He was a huge fish—maybe six feet long, blue skin mottled with pink spots. His fins looked like small, squat legs. He was so ugly he commanded respect. He looked like he was from another time, prehistoric and barely preserved. Cracked with age, he appeared fragile, like the worn sheepskin pages of a rare old book. But the strangest thing about him was the bubble of water encircling his entire body.

"Are you an alien?" Sam asked.

"I beg your pardon?"

"Are you from another planet?"

"This is *my* planet, my world. My kind have been here much longer than yours. At least 170 million years longer. You people thought we were extinct once, but we're not. How dare you ask such a question?"

"What are you then?"

"I am a **coelacanth** from the Comoro Islands off the eastern coast of Africa. My job is protector of my family and teacher of the young. I am very old." He puffed out his gills. "You may call me Jacob."

"But that bubble of water, it's like, like . . ." Sam had no idea what it was like.

"Like magic!" Dapper finished her sentence. "It's his magical motor car!"

Jacob tried to laugh but only gurgled instead. "I suppose that's right. It lets me move around down here so I may watch over everyone. I didn't need this bubble when I lived in the Comores, in my home."

"If you are from this Comores place, what are you doing here? What is this place?" Sam asked.

Jacob stared at her with those cloudy, hooded eyes of his. He seemed to study her very soul. And as he stared, the expression on his blotchy old face seemed to change from doubt to certainty. From sternness to gentleness. "I will answer your questions," he finally said. "You are in the World Beyond the Waves. It is a very special world and you must promise to protect it. You must promise to be brave while you are here. Are you brave?"

"Of course she's brave," said Dapper. "Not as brave as I. But brave. She knows of loss. She dreams of sad things. She would not hurt us, Jacob."

So Jacob began the story of how the World Beyond the Waves was created. "Hundreds of years ago people began to intrude upon our world, the sea. And sea creatures started dying in numbers greater than ever before. Strange things littered the ocean. Deadly things—metal, garbage, sewage. Over the years, they piled higher and thicker, creating a murky sludge on the surface and choking life on the sea floor. Then harpoons pierced the waves, wounding and killing, tearing families apart. The big nets followed, sweeping away millions of animals and destroying their homes. Terrifying new sounds exploded on the surface. Motors, boats, and bombs.

"Then one day, the first black death poured into the sea, crawling over miles of water. Some animals tried to escape through the oil slick, but most died in great pain. Since then, hundreds of oil spills have darkened the oceans, hanging like black clouds, oozing and bleeding into the depths."

Dapper paced, trying to hide his sorrow. So many of his kind —petrels, gulls, other birds—had been downed by the sticky oil, unable to fly. They fluttered helplessly on the surface, their feathers soaked with the poison.

"Sea creatures shared these stories of horror with each other. Their migrations brought news of an increasingly clever, terrifying enemy. That enemy was man," Jacob said.

"Not so long ago, the elders of the sea decided something must be done before all was lost forever. A protected place would be created. A place where ocean animals, injured by the cruelty or foolishness of humans, could find peace, where they could recover. A hospital of sorts. A place where animals on the edge of extinction could go, to search for a mate, in the hope of beginning again."

It was the place where Sam now sat, the World Beyond the Waves.

"Are you hurt? Is that why you're here?" Sam asked.

"I am one of the last of my kind. My wife was captured in 1973. She had five of our babies inside her, waiting to be born. I lost them all. So few of us, and a whole generation gone . . . " Jacob looked away. "I could not protect my family, but I can help protect and teach others, here."

"Aren't *you* afraid of dying?" Sam asked, too overwhelmed to think of anything but this sad and wise creature before her.

"No," Jacob said, without any hesitation. "Dying is part of natural life. When we die the way we are supposed to die, we provide life for others. We provide food for others so they may continue on." Jacob stopped. He looked again at Sam and a shadow crossed his eyes.

"I am afraid, however," he said, "of you, your kind." How could this crusty old fish, here in his world, be afraid of Sam, a girl, a stranger here?

"I am afraid for you, too." Jacob said. "Unless humans stop hurting the world so much, you will destroy everything. Including yourselves."

"I don't understand any of this," Sam said. "What am I doing here?"

"You are here to heal."

Sam touched the bump on her head. How was she going to heal in this cave under the sea? Who was going to make her better? Surely not this old fish in his water bubble and her vain little tropic bird. Was she going to be able to breathe in this air much longer? What if she were really trapped down here?

"You are here to heal and once you have healed, the way home will be there for you," Jacob continued.

"How do I find the way out? I want to go home *now*."

"You will go, Sam, when you are ready. Answers come when you least expect them. All you have to do is look."

CHAPTER FIVE

LIFE SPRINGS FORTH

FIND THE ANSWERS. Find the answers. How was Sam going to find the answers if she didn't even know which questions to ask. She still couldn't understand where she was, how she got there, and how these animals could speak. She was frightened but a little excited too. Excited because she knew she was a part of something no one else was. This was her adventure and hers alone. She could tell stories about it later and everyone would be amazed. She would be special. She decided she would find out what she could about her new friends.

"We had birds in our backyard at home. But they didn't look like you," Sam said to Dapper.

"Of course not. They're just common land birds. I'm a sea bird. I live in the tropics and you won't find anyone as beautiful as I, anywhere. I am the envy of all. I thought I explained that already." Dapper jumped at the chance to be the center of Sam's attention. He told her all about his adventures at sea, his baby brothers, parents, and sister.

"You have a sister?"

"Why yes. Nothing like you, of course. She's very small and not very bright. Sisters usually aren't."

"That's not true," said Sam. "Anyway, you're lucky to have a big family.

I don't have any brothers or sisters." Or parents, Sam thought, but couldn't bring herself to say it.

"Maybe. But everyone's too busy for me. My sister's married now and has no time to play. My parents are too busy looking after my younger brothers, and they have no time to play either. So I went looking for something to do, some fun. That's when I found you and your funny boat with those annoying sails."

"Won't your parents miss you?"

"I know how to take care of myself. I'm very smart and very resourceful. I told them that before I left."

"My aunt and uncle must be missing *me*. Are you sure they're all right?"

"Quite sure," Jacob spoke up. He had been watching the two young beings the whole time.

"How do you know? I mean, aren't we in a cave or something way beneath the surface, way beneath their boat? How could you know how they are?"

"Just as Dapper told you, animals know things. You will have to trust me."

Trust. That was a difficult word for Sam. She had trusted her parents to be there for her. Now they were gone. She had trusted her aunt and uncle to look after her. But they had sailed right into a storm and now they were gone—from her—too. Maybe she really didn't want to go back to them, because up there she couldn't trust anything. Maybe, she thought, she would just stay here and explore this peculiar place forever. She was curious to see more.

"Jacob, if this is a hospital for animals, where are they? There's no one here but us."

"Oh, there are many more here."

"Will you show me? Please."

"Come, then. You should feel well enough to see."

Sam tottered to her feet and rubbed her back. She was stiff but the pounding in her head was not as bad as it had been. Dapper turned and pattered to the back of the room, then disappeared through the floor. Jacob floated after him and suddenly he too was gone. "Come," Jacob said, his voice echoing from somewhere beneath. "Follow me."

Sam took one step, then another, and fell feet first into a hole. The hole opened into a large tunnel, dripping with water and smelling of centuries of sea life. She could stand up to her full height. Dapper was already several yards ahead.

"Come," Dapper said. "We don't have all day." Nonetheless, he paused to rub his tail against the rock. "Ah, best scratching post down here."

Jacob gurgled in annoyance, but waited until the bird had finished showing off. "Sam," he said, "please do not forget to be brave. And remember, I am here to guide you. To teach you. Ask me anything you want."

"You sound like my father. He would have said that," Sam smiled. Jacob smiled more.

Sam, Dapper, and Jacob moved several yards ahead and as they went, the tunnel opened wider and wider. Sam could see light from the far end and she was drawn by its force. Strange sounds grew louder with every step she took. The tunnel ended at a mass of hanging seaweed. When Sam parted the curtain, the sounds abruptly stopped. She drew in her breath as the sight before her was too wondrous to believe. Sam entered the biggest, most glorious landscape she could have imagined. A giant cave stretched further than her eyes could see. Green light from an unknown source danced off the walls. And the walls! They rose like towers of rock, broken by deep cracks and odd-shaped bumps. Dark alcoves and passageways headed off, in every direction, from the main cave. **Stalagmites** reached like giant teeth from the floor. **Stalactites** hung like heavy icicles from the roof, dripping from their tips. Hundreds and hundreds of pools of water lay before her. Huge, glistening boulders rose from the surface of many.

But what had made the sounds? Except for the drip and glug of water, Sam saw nothing that could have made those peculiar noises she'd heard from the tunnel.

"It's all right. You can stop hiding," Jacob called into the hollowness of the cave. Dapper jumped up and down impatiently.

The movements started so slowly Sam only sensed their presence. The pools seemed full, suddenly, of some unknown life. The water stirred. A splash here and there startled the silence. Then all at once, the cave erupted in a rush of activity and sound. Sam stood agog at the life before her. It was everywhere. Sea creatures of all types, sizes and shapes moved and bleeped, glubbed and screeched.

Flying fish sprang from the water and soared through the air. Huge sea mammals climbed onto rocks. Octopus and squid billowed over the bottoms. Turtles bumped into each other, seals pattered beside the walls and opened their mouths under stalactites to catch drips. Porpoises and dolphins frolicked in the froth. Fish, mammals, and wondrous sea creatures appeared as if from nowhere.

A giant clam opened its shell to reveal its soft secrets. Brightly colored fish skated through the streams. Blues and greens and reds and yellows erupted in a brilliant rainbow of life. Great geysers of water spewed out of the far pools.

It was as if the world had just been born all at once. And Sam was there to see it. She couldn't speak. She could barely think. She took a few timid steps into the din. Never, ever, had she known such drama lay hidden beneath the waves. The ocean's surface was really a giant door that opened into another world.

Jacob interrupted her trance and said, "You have a friend down here. Would you like to see him?"

"A friend?" Were there other people down here? Sam couldn't begin to think who she might know in a place like this. Was Jacob playing tricks on her? Sam didn't think he would do that. She followed Jacob deep into the middle of the cavern, through all the movement and sound. She kept searching for someone—something—familiar, but everything she saw was new. Then she spotted him. Her beautiful, wonderful friend. She couldn't stop herself. She ran and ran, closer to this special friend. But when she reached him she halted in her tracks. He was still terribly hurt.

Sam knelt down toward the pool of water, held out her hand, and the dolphin floated into her embrace. It was the dolphin her Uncle Dan had tried to save.

"This is Francis," Jacob said.

"Oh, Francis. I'm sorry we abandoned you. But the storm came and . . . Well, I'm sorry." She stroked his nose and face and he seemed to come alive at her touch. With great effort he opened his mouth and spoke.

"Don't be sorry. I am grateful for everything you did do. You are very kind."

The cut on his side did seem a little better. Sam hoped the medicine her uncle had given him had been enough.

"What can I do to help you now?"

But Francis had struggled so hard to speak, the effort had proved too much. He slipped away, unconscious, his body limp and heavy. Sam looked around desperately for something that would heal the hurt. She was beginning to panic, as all-too-familiar feelings of helplessness overtook her.

"Sam, you can help. You must do as I say," Jacob said.

Dapper began to jump again, looking for attention. But this time there was good reason. He carried two big leaves from a sea plant in his beak.

"You continue to surprise me, little one," said Jacob. "Now Sam, soak those leaves in water, then press them against Francis's wound. Not too hard though."

Sam did as she was told, shaking at first but steady and confident the more she worked. Dapper brought more leaves and Sam made a full bandage for Francis, wrapping it over his wound and around his back.

"Is he going to be okay? My uncle gave him a shot. Will it work?"

"A shot! A shot!" Dapper screeched.

"A shot of *medicine*," Sam said.

"Only time will tell. The next few hours are critical. He must fight the infection from the cut. The medicine and the bandage will help, but Francis must do the rest. We will check on him regularly," Jacob assured her.

"I'm not leaving him. I'm staying right here."

There was such determination in Sam's voice, Jacob did not argue. Sam knew she had to be there with Francis when he woke up. And he would wake up!

Jacob left Sam sitting beside the pool and the injured dolphin. The old coelacanth was never far, though, as Sam caught sight of his bright bubble many times. Dapper sat beside Sam and despite his usual cockiness, remained quiet and watchful too.

Only once did Dapper interrupt the silence. He told Sam how Francis had arrived in the World Beyond the Waves. "He almost didn't make it here, you know. When I landed on your boat and saw how hurt he was, I knew I had to go for help. But before I left, I told Francis to stay near you." So, Sam thought, that's what Dapper had been screeching to the dolphins just before the storm hit! "When I came back, the storm was much worse. It was hard to find Francis. We finally spotted him, but he had been separated from the other two dolphins, his brother and sister."

For hours the girl and the bird sat and watched and waited. All the other animals swam or flew or walked or splashed. But Sam never heard them and Francis never moved. He just floated and breathed so quietly Sam kept checking to see if he was still alive. At one point Francis's tail fluttered and his body jerked. Sam bolted up and began to call his name. But his eyes never opened and he drifted back to his state of frightening stillness.

More hours went by. Sam and Dapper continued to wait. What was so urgent about saving this life, Sam wondered. Her thoughts carried her back to a day before her parents' lives were lost. Her mother had been packing for the trip to Florida. She was looking through the pile of clothes Sam's father had stuffed into his suitcase. Mom had said, "Oh, he's not taking these?!" She had screwed up her nose in mock disgust, holding a pair of grungy sneakers in her hands. Sam knew those were her dad's favorite shoes—broken in by years of wear. Sam used to stand on those shoes, her father's feet inside them, as he walked her around the house, hanging onto her fists and singing the "Humpa Jump" song.

She hummed the tune now, and stroked Francis lightly on his head. "As I went down the humpa jump, the humpa jump a jazzi, I thought I saw a ragmashag eating my capazzi. If I'd a had my rigmatig, my rigmatig ma tazzi—" Then she felt it. The tiniest shudder of life from the dolphin's body.

"Francis. Francis. Wake up."

Francis opened his eyes, stared at Sam, and said, "Thank you."

Great big tears of happiness poured down Sam's cheeks. Jacob came from somewhere close by and looked fondly at Francis, satisfied and relieved. Dapper raced back and forth beside the pool, too excited to contain himself.

The water in the dolphin's pool erupted in a sudden spray of life as Francis's younger brother and sister crashed through the surface. They had found him! And they knew he would be all right. Everyone knew it. The infection was gone and Francis acted as if he had never been hurt at all. It was a miracle. Francis turned and swam toward Dorey and Bonnie, his family. The three dolphins played and splashed in sheer delight, drenching Sam in a shower of water. For the first time since she had arrived in this world, Sam found herself laughing.

CHAPTER SIX

SHARK THREAT

THE LAUGHTER WAS a welcome release for Sam. And her joyous sounds were joined by caws and bleeps and cooing from around the colossal cave. Soon a whole chorus of sea music filled the room and the pools, seeming to lift the very floor on which Sam stood. Echoes boomed off the domed ceiling and animals floated on their happy thoughts.

"Oh!" Sam gasped, in between her laughs. She looked with open adoration at the playful creatures dancing in the pool before her.

"Dolphins. They're always showing off," Dapper said, miffed that someone else was stealing the show. Francis and Dorey and Bonnie kicked up a watery fuss, moving together in perfect unison. They leaped high above the surface, leaving hardly a ripple as they rose, curled their sleek forms through the air, and dove back through the water with a mighty splash.

"Silly things," Dapper clucked. "They'll wear themselves out." He almost seemed to pout. He stomped over to the edge of the pool and glared at the dolphins. With that, Francis turned his back to the taunting tropic bird and whacked his tail against the surface, giving Dapper a surprise shower. Francis swam over to the drenched bird and poked him in the stomach.

"Who's stupid now?" Francis teased, his black eyes gleaming. It was hard for Sam to imagine this creature anything but playful as his long lower jaw and curved mouth made him look like he was always grinning.

Sam knew what was hidden behind that grin. She knew Francis had suffered. But she still didn't know what had caused his injury. Gently, slowly, she asked the dolphin what had hurt him. But before Francis could speak, Jacob appeared again, as was his habit, and coaxed Sam away from the pool's edge. He said, "Francis knows what happened, but his brother and sister are too young to understand. It is better not to tell them this way, for they may become too afraid to return to the outside world. Dolphins are one of the most sensitive of all sea creatures."

"What did happen?" Sam asked.

"They were swimming, looking for a meal of squid and shellfish, when the entire world around them was swept into a net. A **drift net** hanging from a boat. Their parents and three others in their group were drowned as the net strangled around them. Francis found a hole in the net. But the hole was small and the nylon cut Francis as he pushed his way out. Bonnie and Dorey followed. They probably would have been killed had they been caught, and probably slowly and painfully. You do not need to know how."

"Why were they caught?" Sam asked.

"That is the saddest part," said Jacob. "The fishermen were catching tuna for people to eat. Dolphins, whales, turtles, and many other animals get caught in the drift nets along with the tuna. They are injured or killed and merely thrown back overboard like so much garbage. They feel pain. They feel pain just like you do. They bleed just like you do."

"What will happen to the dolphins now, Jacob? Do they have to leave or can they stay? I want them to stay."

"They will stay until Francis is ready to go. He can teach his brother and sister the lessons of the sea, in safety, while they are here."

"How can they learn about the sea in here? These are just pools of water. This isn't the ocean," Sam asked, looking around her.

"No. But we may reach the ocean easily," Jacob said. "There are passageways through the pools so all the sea creatures may come and go as they please. Francis can take the younger ones out every day and teach them how to comb the waters for food. Things their mother would have taught. One day they will go and not come back."

Sam now knew why she felt a special bond with Francis. They were both orphans. His happy face and sad story told of such courage. She looked at him then, and he looked back with open eyes and an open heart. "I don't want him to go. He'll die out there," she said. "Make them stay, Jacob."

"They cannot stay forever, Sam. Their home is the sea. They swim miles every day, following whales, surfing on waves, hunting, playing."

"And they're pretty tasty, too." A new voice purred from another pool beside Sam. She whirled around and jumped back from the edge. She knew this creature too. She had read stories, bad stories, about the things it did. It hurt people.

"I hope *you* go." Sam turned to Jacob for support, but he, in his usual style, had left her again. The **silky shark's** small pig-eyes stared Sam down. It spun its nine-foot, 300-pound body with startling speed and sliced through the water like a razor, moving away from Sam. She shuddered with relief.

Dapper was pacing around the edge of the dolphin pool, clucking at Francis. Sam stepped backwards to avoid the tropic bird but as she did, her deck shoes lost their grip and she slipped. Sam's feet flew out from under her and she fell in a tangle of waving limbs through the surface of the shark pool. Her frantic arms were churning up the water. Sam grabbed for the edge but her hands only slipped off the smooth rocks. Francis began to yell. He was saying something. He was telling her to be still. Sam obeyed, her trust in Francis growing from a place in her she did not yet understand. Then Francis dove deep and disappeared.

The water in the shark's pool lay in a dead calm. Sam searched the depths for movement. Nothing stirred. She waited, thick terror choking her. The air seemed to throb with tension. Dapper was as still as a stuffed animal as he stood by, watching Sam. His eyes were glassy.

Dapper heard it before Sam. He started to screech. The water was moving. Something below was pushing at it, coming closer. Sam felt the ripples shift. Something brushed her leg. This was it. This was the end. A dark shape, a large form, circled beneath her. She sensed it but never saw it. It moved away, turned, and in a terrifying burst of energy it came at her, plowing through depths with a force and aim too great to escape. The water rushed at her. Sam closed her eyes and opened her mouth, her scream overpowering all else. Then it hit. The lights went out.

"I think maybe she's fainted," Dapper said, hovering over Sam, his beak practically in her nose.

"Gosh, I didn't mean to scare her." Francis's concern shadowed his eyes.

"What . . . what happened?" Sam asked, coming to on the ground beside the shark pool.

"I'm sorry," said Francis, "I just wanted to get you out."

Sam thought she would faint again, this time from relief. "I thought you were the shark."

"I know. I'm sorry. I just wanted to help." Francis lowered his eyes, then dove again, returning to his own pool.

"You saved my life. You really saved my life. Thank you."

Sam looked at her special friend with love she knew she could never begin to show. They had saved each other, and their bond grew stronger still.

"Oh, I don't really think your life was in danger," Francis said.

"*Excuse* me." The shark was back and casting a less-than-pleased glare over Sam and Francis.

"This is Sito the silky shark." Dapper piped up. "And although he'd like you to believe otherwise, he's never tasted a human. He eats **groupers** and **snappers**. He's terribly ugly, yes, but you shouldn't be so hard on him. In fact, he was caught by the same drift net as Francis. The fishermen threw him on board and cut him before they tossed him back."

The distress on Sam's face melted into confusion. Dapper flapped his wings and circled Sito's pool. When Sito neared the surface, Dapper hovered over his silver form and landed on his back just behind his **dorsal fin**.

"Get off me, you pest," Sito snapped.

"Not until you tell her," said Dapper, "or shall I?"

Dapper looked over at Sam and winked. "He's probably embarrassed to tell you. He wants us all to think he's so fierce. He . . ."

"Shut up," Sito growled.

"Sito's not so tough. He's been beaten now, twice at least. Once by humans with their net . . ."

Sito spun around the pool trying to rid himself of the pesky bird. As he turned, Sam saw the cuts only a knife could have made. Sito's injured body must have been causing him more pain than his injured pride, Sam realized.

"And he was beaten one other time, when Francis was born," Dapper continued. "Sito and five other sharks tried to crowd in on Francis's mother as she was giving birth. A mother having a baby is a very easy target. She can't protect herself. But several big male dolphins came to her rescue. They circled around Francis's mother and jabbed at the sharks, fighting them off. Were they ever surprised!" Dapper winked.

Francis spoke from the other pool. "My father and uncles chased the leader of the group, a great white shark, and jabbed it in the belly until it left. The other sharks, including Sito, turned tail and swam away." The three dolphins clapped their flippers on the water in applause.

Sito twisted and thrashed, trying to toss the bothersome bird from his back, and finally dove away in disgust.

"So misunderstood," Dapper teased, as he landed on the rocks again. "Sharks do seem to eat anything. Or at least they try to. They feast on things like license plates, the leftovers from the other animals' meals, anything. But just because they're not fussy eaters is no reason for your kind," he pointed his wing at Sam, "to hate them and hunt them down. We tropic birds have much more refined tastes than sharks, of course. Most animals do. But, well, think of sharks as vacuum cleaners. They suck up all the garbage down here and the rest of us are quite glad they do."

"Well, I'm still scared of him," said Sam, but her features had softened and she spoke with a little less conviction.

"Hey, you won't find me presenting myself on a platter for him either," said Dapper. "If Sito had more than a pea brain in his head, I'm sure he would be more afraid of you than you are of him."

CHAPTER SEVEN

Deadly Intruder

AT THE END of her first day in the World Beyond the Waves, Sam realized how hungry she was. She asked Jacob what she could eat, and he set Francis and Dapper to work collecting a vast array of plants. They came in all shapes and sizes, from little round morsels to big maroon leaves. Her friends laid the food out to dry, and when it was ready, they presented their great feast with glowing pride.

"Ick." Sam wrinkled her nose. "You don't expect me to eat that!"

Francis looked hurt and tucked his nose beneath the water.

Dapper's yellow tail drooped as he stuttered, "It's . . . it's the best we've got."

"I just can't. I'm sorry but it's not what I eat. My food is cooked. It doesn't look anything like this." Sam retreated into a corner, feeling slightly ashamed. She found a bed of seaweed and lowered herself down, throwing her jacket over her. She thought her stomach grumbles would keep her up, but before she knew it, Sam had drifted to sleep, exhausted by the overwhelming events of the day.

Several hours later, Sam's hunger pangs prodded her awake. As soon as she was able to focus, she sat up. Something was wrong. The air was electric with tension and fear. All the animals were as still as they could be, motionless on the rocks or hovering in the water. She looked frantically around for Francis or Dapper. She spotted the dolphins, alert but still, in their pool. But she couldn't see the tropic bird.

"Dapper, where are you?" A wing closed over her mouth.

"Shhhh," he said, stepping up beside her. "Listen and don't move."

Sam strained her ears, but all she could hear was water dripping into the pools and the occasional whoosh of breath from the sea mammals. She waited.

Then it came. First one, then another, then another. Closer still. Whomph. Whomph. Whomph. Hollow thudding sounds, from somewhere outside the cave, entered their world. She heard several more whomphs in the next half hour, and all the while she just stared, eyes wide open, at the stillness before her. Her stomach let out a loud rumble once, and she gasped. But whatever was making those sounds seemed not to have heard her. Finally the strange noises stopped, but the silence was almost worse. Sam and the animals continued to wait. Jacob moved with the stealth of a shadow among the group and spoke.

"I believe it's gone," he said in a voice barely above a whisper, "for now."

The animals all unlocked their taut muscles. They slipped away to their activities once again but with slow, tame movements. Sam hurried over to Francis, Dapper flapping along behind her. The dolphin swam toward her, and they touched each other for reassurance.

"What was it?" Sam asked. There was more fear in her voice than she had intended. "A human sound, whatever it was," Francis said. Sam didn't know how to react. She felt at once anger at whoever had done that but also a great longing to be with them, her own kind. She felt a gnawing loneliness creep over her.

"Maybe they were looking for me," Sam offered. "Maybe I should go."

Jacob floated in his mystical bubble right up to Sam's pale face. She expected him to object, but he said nothing, just kept staring, then he moved on.

"You should go back to sleep," Dapper said. "As long as you're awake, I'm awake, and I'm tired."

"Are you baby-sitting me?" Sam asked. "I'm not a baby. I don't need to be guarded."

"I have better things to do than baby-sit girls," Dapper clucked. "I just want to make sure you don't go wandering off and get yourself—or someone else—in trouble." She was about to protest but Dapper had turned his back to her and she gave up.

"Fine," she said.

"Fine," he said.

Francis looked with amusement at the squabbling girl and bird. He pushed his nose against Sam's hand as she settled down beside his pool, Dapper leaning against her leg. Then the three of them sighed on the same beat.

Resigned and cloaked in a temporary peace, they all fell back to sleep. Three friends, all different, yet all the same. Francis on one side, Dapper on the other, and Sam in the middle.

Light seeped through Sam's eyelids, and she awoke yawning. She started to sit up but immediately remembered the fright from the middle of the night and checked to make sure everything was okay. The sounds and movements seemed normal enough, so Sam got up. Was she hungry now! Francis was still asleep. She searched the room for Dapper, but he was nowhere to be found.

"Some guard," Sam muttered to herself.

No one paid her any attention as she hurried over to her spread of food. It was all still there, and it still looked disgusting to Sam. But hunger can make anything seem appetizing. She reached gingerly at first, then grabbed at the plants, stuffing them into her mouth. She chewed, gagged, almost spit them out, but forced herself to swallow. They tasted bitter and salty. Nothing like the pizza for which her mouth watered. She was poking around the rest of the food when Dapper said, "Tasty, aren't they?" He bobbed his head, eyes teasing, into her view.

"Why are you always doing that? Coming up behind me?"

Dapper ignored her question. "So I see you aren't too prim and proper, too ladylike, after all," Dapper said. He pointed with his beak to Sam's hands and face, which were covered in the remains of the meal.

"Just go away," Sam said. She had been caught in quite a mess.

"As you wish."

Dapper flew over to Sito the shark and they both began whispering and chuckling, looking over every so often in Sam's direction. Her face grew hot with anger. Several minutes later Dapper flew back.

"Sito says you have worse eating habits than he has." Sam had had enough. She marched over to Sito's pool and this time stood right over the edge, defying him to come closer. He did, and Sam held her ground.

"Maybe *you're* not a monster," Sam said, "but other sharks, great white sharks, are man-eaters."

"What do you expect?"

"What do I expect?" Sam asked, shocked.

"You make these so-called beaches and just declare them off limits to sharks. Like we're supposed to know or something. There aren't any walls out in the ocean. There aren't any signs saying 'No sharks allowed.' Besides, you just take over blocks of the sea as if you owned it. This is our home. We live here and we hunt and eat here. If a human gets hurt while trespassing in our territory, you all get mad. You go hunting for us. I've seen how you do that!" Sito said. "And when you humans catch us, you laugh. You hang us on display so others can gawk and poke at us. We don't do that. That's mean."

"I never thought about it that way before," Sam said, subdued now.

"You just never thought, period. All you care about are furry little animals and pretty little dolphins. You call them cute. You try to make them human. When you look at us you decide we're ugly. Why? For trying to make the world a cleaner place? Just stay out of my way." Sito gnashed the air with his jaws, trying to impress with his rows of pointed teeth. But his attempt at a ferocious demon fell far short. All Sam saw was a big, goofy grin. She laughed. Sito gulped and burped. "As I said, you stay out of our way, and we'll stay out of yours." Sito spun away with a defiant twist and sawed through the water. Sam watched, laughter and respect tickling the corners of her mouth.

With Sito ignoring her, Sam decided to look in on Francis. She took two steps when commotion suddenly erupted behind her. She whirled around and gasped. The ground rumbled as water in a pool across the room was sucked back into the ocean beyond, leaving an empty crater. Then a giant geyser spurted upwards, like the breath of a dragon, spewing seaweed and a small bundle of whiskers and fur into the cave. The crater filled again with water and on its edge a small sea lion lay whimpering and writhing.

Sam and Dapper rushed over to the animal and Sam wanted to cry. The sea lion was strangling on a choker of plastic fishing net and other debris. Sam knelt closer. There were rings from six-packs and pieces of plastic bags entangled around the pup's throat. Sam reached down and began to pull the garbage apart, trying to remove it from the animal's neck. Her heart broke. The pup gasped and cried a sorrowful cry. He opened his mouth and struggled for air. Sam worked faster but her hands fumbled through the mess. The harder she pulled, the tighter it knotted.

"Oh, no," Sam whispered. "Please hang on." She pulled again at the tattered garbage but it held fast. "Someone help me," she pleaded. Francis circled around and around in his pool, crying louder than the sea lion. No one else moved. They seemed quiet, resigned, as if they had seen this many times before. As Sam frantically clawed at the debris, the pup's huge, deep eyes looked up at her, reflecting all the pain and bewilderment of the world. *Why*, he seemed to ask. Then he died.

Sam looked down at the beautiful creature she cradled in her arms, his body limp, his little head curled against her chest. She sat like that for a long time. Finally, the pain of her own loss welled inside her, and her body shook with sobs. The tears would not stop. The little sea lion and Sam were locked in an embrace of life and love and death that was the end for one, the beginning for the other. Why weren't the babies of the world protected? Somewhere in the distance she thought she heard Jacob say, "Leave her be. Her time has come."

Dapper was unusually quiet as Sam finally let the baby sea lion go. Francis pushed the baby's body down through the secret waterways and out to sea. He came back to stay as close to Sam as he could. There was nothing he could say. Sam withdrew from her friends and watched, her expression blank, as the other animals went back to their business. They had seen this many times before, Sam later discovered. Thousands of these curious animals get trapped in plastic garbage every year. Battling for every breath, they suffocate for days, sometimes weeks, dying an agonizing death.

Jacob approached some time later. "Thank you," he said, simply.

"For what? He died. Everyone around me dies."

"Eventually, yes," said Jacob.

"Leave me alone. I don't want to talk to you. I don't want to be here any more. You're all sick or hurt and you show me your pain as if I can help. I can't help. I can't do anything. And you can't do anything for me."

"Come now," Jacob gently scolded. "You're just feeling sorry for yourself. You didn't make him die. You tried to help. And you *did* help Francis." Sam turned her face away and stared at a world beyond the cave walls. Jacob turned to leave, but before he went he said, "You didn't make your parents die either." Sam whirled her head around but Jacob was gone. Of course she didn't make her parents die. But they died anyway. They left her. Everyone leaves her.

CHAPTER EIGHT

ORCA SONG

AFTERNOON CAME AND Sam was again hungry. This time she didn't object as Dapper laid out a meal much like the one she had eaten earlier. She ate well. Francis had taken his brother and sister out to sea to look for their own food. Sam was worried for their safety but knew she couldn't protect them.

"Let's go play," said Dapper.

"I don't want to play," said Sam. This was not a place for play, Sam thought. Not play, or fun, or games. It was a place for growing up.

"Those are my orders." Dapper pecked at Sam until she stood up.

"I'll watch you play," she said. Sam didn't want to grow up too fast.

Dapper found an octopus bumping into the corners of its shallow sea bed. Dapper poked his head under the water for a better look. Eight-legged Lilly had tied herself in a knot.

"Oh dear, oh my, whatever shall I do?" Lilly kept colliding into the pool walls as she turned around and around. "Oh dear, oh me."

This comic sight was too much for Dapper to resist. He jumped into the pool, tucked his wings, and paddled toward the mishap. Dapper kept ducking, poking, then surfacing. Finally, after several "Oh my's" and "Good grief's," Lilly's knotted legs came undone. In an act of thanks, she threw her many legs around the startled tropic bird and gave him a big hug. When Dapper emerged again, he was wearing Lilly on his head.

"All right, all right, Lilly," Dapper said, smothering in her hug. Sam could hardly make out his muffled words. Lilly gave the squirming bird one final squeeze, then she was off, moving in a ballet of freedom.

Dapper scampered onto the land, shook himself, and walked away without another word. He led Sam to the far side of the cave, past Sito the shark, who was displaying his magnificent teeth to an audience of two seals. He stopped at an immense pool. Sam, despite herself, peered in.

"There's nothing here," she said.

"Maybe. Maybe not."

"Is this a game? I'm supposed to guess what's down here?"

"Not at all,"said Dapper. "You won't need to guess."

Curiosity overtook Sam, and she watched and waited. The seconds turned into minutes. She thought she caught a movement somewhere from the depths, but nothing came, the water only rippling slightly.

"I'm going." Sam was now more nervous than curious.

Just as she stood up to leave, a shape emerged, black, awesome. It rose with the force and power and stealth of a submarine. Then it was gone. Sam froze, wanting to run, unable to move her feet. In a burst of sound and water and speed, the giant reared out of the darkness and hurled its body up into the air, crashing down with a deafening blow through the surface.

"That's Nicky. Nicky's come out to play," Dapper sang, teasing Sam as she shook the water off herself and found that she had jumped several feet back.

"Here, Nicky, Nicky," Dapper nattered, swishing his wing on the pool surface. Nicky's reply was not what Dapper expected. A belch of air shot straight out of the pool and knocked the little bird off his feet.

"You act like a human," Nicky said then, his massive nose now poking through the water. Sam had seen creatures like this in movies, but up close he was much more spectacular. Nicky was a young **orca**, a killer whale. His eyes were wide and watchful, hinting at the strong spirit beneath. His tall dorsal fin pointed proudly heavenward, halos of white painted on either side of his head. When Nicky saw Sam, he submerged again.

"Nicky, it's okay. Sam's my friend. She's not like the rest of them," Dapper said. Sam looked on, confused. Nicky flicked up the water with his tail and stuck the tip of his snout out again.

"It's okay, really." This time Sam tried to encourage the timid animal. He floated higher then and opened his massive mouth. A tongue, the color of pink pillows, curled over his teeth. His words, when they came, seemed to float on a wave of violins.

"Come," he said. Sam stepped near.

"Closer," he said. Sam knelt down. Then he bounced his head as if nodding approval and said, "Play with me."

"With you? How would I play with you?"

"Jump in. I'll show you."

Sam didn't move. There was no way, ever, she was going to get into the water with that animal, as gentle as he seemed. But before she knew what had happened, a cold wet nose had pushed her from behind and Sam was in. She splashed and kicked and looked up to see who had pushed her. It was one of the seals she had noticed near Sito. Nicky dipped and turned and came up underneath Sam, who was struggling to grab hold of the slippery rocks. But Nicky carried her off, and he swam around in circles, Sam on his back. She actually began to enjoy herself. Like a day at the amusement park. He whirled and circled again, piercing through the water like a 25-foot torpedo, and Sam shrieked with happiness. Nicky submerged and Sam swam beside him until her legs turned to rubber. Then Nicky nudged her with his nose and prodded her up beside the pool, where she lay gasping and laughing. The 7,000-pound Nicky was no more of a threat to Sam than the puppy she once owned.

"Can you do tricks?" Sam asked, inspired by the memory of Dixy, her terrier, who used to roll over and beg. Nicky's eyes clouded, shielding the hurt beneath, and he submerged without the hint of an answer.

"Can he?" said Dapper. "He can jump and spin and clap his flippers and speak, all on command."

"Well, why won't he then?"

"Why won't *you*?" asked Nicky as he reappeared. "I don't think you'd find it very dignified to be forced to do stupid tricks just to get your dinner." Sam learned Nicky had been held captive in a marine park where he was told to perform tricks to groups of people.

"The owners of the marine park kidnapped me from my family," Nicky said. "I have a mother and father, sisters, brothers, uncles, cousins, and aunts. I could hear them calling for me as I was being taken. I could hear them for miles."

"But, didn't the people at the marine park take care of you? Weren't you well treated?" Sam asked.

"The best treatment in any prison doesn't change the fact it's still a prison. And a small one at that. In my pod—my group—we travel thousands of miles every year. I was put in a one-hundred-foot tank. With no family. But I survived. I had the satisfaction of knowing that, as ridiculous as they made me appear, the spectators who were clapping and screeching looked more foolish than I."

Who was a spectator of whom, Sam wondered. "How did you get out?"

"That will remain my secret. I will never go back. I would die first. We orcas are the greatest hunters of the sea. We used to fear nothing, not even the great white shark. Yet now I fear what people can do. You see us as toys. I am not a toy."

"If you are such great hunters, why do you get captured? Why don't you attack people?"

"Because we share something very special with humans. My grandfather explained it to me. He told me the great legend of our birth. Once upon a time, he said, orcas all used to be common dolphins. We are part of the dolphin family, you see. But many years ago, a human child fell into the sea. The child was cold and frightened, and her cries were like the cries of our young. Two dolphins tried to rescue the child by cradling her between their backs as they floated side by side beneath her. But the dolphins were too small to hold her for long. They were filled with despair, for they knew the child would drown. But suddenly, a warm light shone down on the dolphins and the girl. A song began to play: 'I am the sea. Don't cry for me. Make your bodies strong. Take me along. Pure black and white. Fly through the night.' When the light went out, the dolphins had turned into orcas, strong and black and white. They carried the girl to shore in the middle of the night."

Sam dared not speak. She dared not think. That story. That song...

"So you see, we are connected in a special way to humans," Nicky continued. "We couldn't hurt you. But you hurt us. Why?"

Sam reached out with tenderness and touched Nicky's halo just above his left eye.

"I would never hurt you," she said. "And I will never forget you." Nicky rubbed his nose against Sam's hand, looked at her one last time, then disappeared into the depths. Sam knew he had left, gone to look for his family. It was time she left, she decided, to look for hers.

"Jacob," Sam called, "Jacob." He came, floating above the rocks. "Jacob, I want to go. I want to go home."

"You will find the way yourself. When you are ready."

"When will I be ready?" Her question was interrupted with a splash, as Francis, Bonnie, and Dorey swirled through the air and plunged back into their pool.

"You're back," Sam cried, her concern for the dolphins evaporating in a mist of affection.

"Yes," said Francis. "We left to get food but as we neared the surface we saw three shadows overhead. Three ships. Two small ones and a big, big one. We explored. But I don't know what they were doing."

"Ships!" Sam said. "One of those must be my aunt and uncle's boat. They're looking for me. They must be worried. I have to go."

"And go you will," Jacob said. "Look for the way with your heart, not your eyes."

Sam felt cross. She didn't understand Jacob and his riddles. "Tell me how. Now!"

All Jacob said was, "The answers are there."

CHAPTER NINE

CRIES OF THE
SEA CREATURES

SAM'S SECOND NIGHT was no calmer than the first. She tossed and turned, then decided to get up and sit by Francis's pool, letting the soft slap of the water and his presence lull her to sleep. But as she arose, she heard sounds, like dampened voices, from a small alcove off the cave. Sam remembered the sounds her parents had often made, after she had gone to bed. They had spoken in hushed tones, sometimes with anger or worry. She used to crawl to the top step and listen to her parents below, but their words often made no sense. Sam crawled now to the wall off the alcove and, like a little girl, huddled in silence as the whispers drifted by.

"She's not ready yet." It was Jacob's voice.

"Are you certain?" a deep voice asked, one she had not heard before.

"Yes. I am certain. Soon, though, very soon."

"Is she the right one?"

"She will help us when she goes back to her world. But she is just not ready yet."

"You know what will happen if you are wrong."

With a start, Sam realized they were talking about her. She craned her neck around the wall but all she could see was the coelacanth in his transparent bubble. Nothing else. No one else.

Sam crawled silently back to the dolphin pool and laid herself down beside the edge, her hand trailing through the water, her jacket rolled up under her head.

Morning came and Sam had a strong feeling it was the start of a special day, a day like no other. This vague sense that something important was going to happen made her restless. It made her itch. She pulled on all her reserve to be patient. It was hard.

She needed to see more, she needed the answers. She leaned toward Francis and gently prodded him. "Wake up, wake up."

"Good morning, Sam. Why do you look so anxious?"

"Are people really bad?" she whispered. "Do we hurt everything in the ocean?"

"*You're* not bad. Many people aren't, I suppose. I guess you just don't realize what your world does to our world."

"You mean things like oil spills and drift nets. Or plastic garbage." Sam's heart lost a beat. "I learned about those things in school, but I really didn't understand how much damage they do. I didn't know you then. Or Nicky, or...I just didn't realize."

Sam put her feet in the water and faced Francis. "I guess it's hard, living in a city, to really appreciate how much the animals of the sea, or any animals, suffer. We learn about it from a distance. We don't feel very close to it, we don't make it *our* problem. I feel so ashamed."

"I guess that's the trouble with humans. You've changed the world so much you've forgotten what really matters. You've forgotten to pass on the important messages. Things that we animals pass on to our children, generation after generation. We tell our children they can only take what they need. That we all must give as much as we take. We don't understand things like 'greed' or 'impatience.' Soon people will have taken so much, destroyed so much, there won't be anything left. You've got to stop this madness." Francis knew his words had deeply affected Sam, as tears welled in her eyes. He rested his nose on her knees to comfort her. But Sam pulled her feet out of the pool and stood up.

"That plastic around the baby sea lion's neck—it could have been garbage I threw away. The net that cut you—maybe I ate the tuna from that catch. Oh, Francis, what are we doing to all of you?"

"I'm not going to tell you it's okay. It's not. But there is a lot you can do. I knew you were special when I first saw you. All children are special. You still have hope. We've been waiting for someone like you to help us. To start spreading the truth. We're relying on you, and other young people, to do the right thing. We trust you."

Sam was disturbed by everything she had seen, everything Francis had said. She was afraid she couldn't do enough to help. Yet she was drawn to the creatures and their stories by a tugging, invisible cord. Sam struggled with her thoughts, feeling shame, confusion, and a great longing to do *something*. But when she turned to look into Francis's eyes, the struggle stopped. She knew then what she had to do. She reached into the water, hugged the dolphin around his neck, and said, "I will learn everything I can about your world. You can trust me."

"I love you, Sam," Francis said.

"I love you, too. I love all of you." Sam threw her arms into the air, as if giving all the animals in the cave a big hug. Dapper suddenly appeared from the shadows, as he often seemed to do, and flew onto her shoulder.

"Come on, Dapper, we have work to do. Show me all you can here. Tell me all there is to tell."

So off they went. Sam met a **sturgeon** couple. Their grey coloring made them appear older than they were. The female was crying. Her four-foot body shook. "She won't have babies," the smaller male said, "and she wants them very much."

"Why doesn't she just have them, then?" Sam asked.

"She's afraid her eggs would be taken for caviar," he said, "and I'm afraid, too. People take the eggs before they are laid. Then I would lose my babies and my wife."

Sam met a **blue marlin**, a sleek, beautiful animal that dipped and swirled like a kite. His pointed nose protruded like a flag pole from his pool. But his lovely face was damaged, twisted into a grotesque grin, by a hook sticking out of his mouth. "People play a game with us. It's a peculiar game. They chase us with big boats and try to catch us. I'm not sure why. I think it's because we're trophies. What's a trophy?"

Sam didn't know how to answer.

"But I outsmarted them," the magnificent marlin said with gloating pride. Neither he nor Sam mentioned the ugly hook.

A crater of muddy water lay before Sam but there appeared to be no life inside. Dapper told Sam there were pearls buried in the mud but when she reached her hand through the slime all she found were oysters. And they were spitting at her.

"Guess they're guarding their pearls pretty tightly today." said Dapper.

"What do you mean? What pearls?"

"Oysters *make* pearls, silly. When sand gets trapped inside their shells, it hurts them. It hurts and rubs and causes pain. So oysters release a special fluid that coats the grain of sand. When it hardens, a pearl is formed. Voila."

"I never knew that," Sam whispered. She remembered the pearl necklaces she'd seen in jewelry store windows and found it hard to imagine such perfect beauty could be created out of painful particles of sand.

Dapper took Sam to a special alcove where dozens of seals stretched their rubbery bodies on the rocks. They looked like plump worms covering the ground after a rain. They made a racket, chattering to each other and jostling for prime space.

"Wow. Why are so many of them here?"

"Their island home was coated with an oil slick. These are the ones that escaped. But they didn't escape without suffering. They have to bathe in clean water every day until all the poisonous oil comes off." Dapper looked so sad and Sam knew he had lost many of his friends this way.

Sam was introduced to the most curious creatures with more curious names. A group of monkfish, freckled with white spots and fringed with a crown of spines, stirred up the mud. A guitar fish hummed through the water, its yellowish flat back beating rhythms as it swam. A catfish crawled the bottoms. Sam saw blonde rays, pointed rays, cuckoo rays. She saw the thorned barndoor skate and the striped clear-nosed skate. The plate-like shape of a stingray combed the bottom of its pool, and Sam thought it so funny she wanted to reach down and tickle it.

"I wouldn't do that if I were you," said Dapper. "He has poison in his tail spine. He could hurt you." Sam jerked her hand back. The small eyes seemed to look up at her with a warning to stay away. His relative, a cow-nosed ray, had no such venom and Sam touched the surface of its diamond-shaped back. She giggled at the shape of its snout.

"What are they doing here?" Sam asked.

"There are poisons much stronger than the poison in a stingray's tail," Dapper said. "All **skates** and **rays** live in muddy shallow water close to shore, where those poisons collect and infect them. You call it pollution."

"What does pollution do to the animals?" Sam asked.

"Talk to Francis. He knows."

Sam, who knew her way around the domed underworld fairly well by now, walked over to the dolphins' pool. "Tell me what pollution does to you."

Francis called his sister Bonnie and she swam up to Sam. Bonnie pointed her long nose into the air and Sam saw something that didn't look quite right. Little holes, like sores, marked the underside of her jaw.

"Pollution kills many sea animals. Sometimes we can see it, often we can't. It can infect our food, and when we eat we get sick. Or worse. Bonnie was lucky." Francis rubbed his beak with fondness against his sister's face.

Sam could see all the factories coughing up smoke, all the garbage dumps leaking their poisons into the ground and eventually to the sea. She remembered as a little girl, her mother had taken her for a picnic by a river. She had asked her mom what the yellow foamy scum was on the river's surface. 'It's pollution,' her mother had answered. 'Who makes it?' Sam had asked. 'We all do,' her mother had said. Sam's first challenge to innocence had left her saddened. 'You mean our family, we make pollution?' 'I try not to,' her mother had said, 'but it's hard. There's not much one person can do to stop it.'

"There's not much one person can do," Sam said aloud, returning to her present thoughts. "I'm just one person. What can I do?"

Neither Francis nor Dapper answered. They left Sam to search for herself.

"What's the point?" Sam said finally. "What's the point!" she shouted, echoes booming off the cave walls.

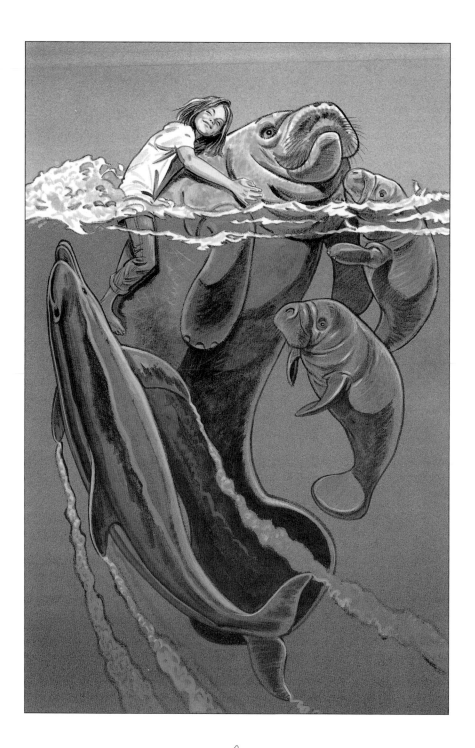

CHAPTER TEN

THE GIFT OF
UNDERSTANDING

AS SOON AS she'd yelled, Sam knew she had made a mistake. Whomph. Whomph. The frightening noise had started again, and it was much closer than the night before. Every animal halted in midmotion, caught in a trance of fear. Only their eyes moved, darting back and forth, hoping they wouldn't see who or what the intruder was. Thuds seemed to be echoing off the chamber itself. They were coming more rapidly now, as if they had hit their target. Then they stopped.

The silence was cold and left the creatures exposed, naked. Were they being watched? Sam stood and waited. Her breath was shallow. Her palms were wet with fear, her mouth dry. Dapper had tucked his beak under his left wing as if shutting out the noise would make it go away. Francis had ducked under the water, hovering protectively over Bonnie and Dorey.

Minutes went by and still no one moved. Sam wondered how long they were going to wait. She needn't have wondered at all.

A loud whirring, like giant eggbeaters, cut through the silence and the sea. The propellers—if that's what they were—seemed to be directly overhead. Clanking followed, as if shards of metal were being thrown against the rocks. Then blasts of sound erupted around them, growing louder, deafening. Something struck the walls of the cave, and the sonic aftershock rained down on the group, exploding in their ears. The rooms seemed to creak and groan like a sinking supertanker. Walls ruptured, particles flew, rocks collapsed. The ground quaked.

Sam covered her ears, Francis shuddered, Dapper tucked his head deeper. Sam knelt and hugged the frightened bird, but he didn't respond.

Out of the corner of her eye, Sam caught a huge sea mammal slipping into a pool. Its body was limp, still. Moments later the explosion stopped. This time, the silence that followed was shattered by cries. Sam was rooted to her spot. Jacob sailed over to the animal Sam had seen.

"Sam," he barked. "Sam, come now."

But Sam was stuck. "Sam!" Jacob roared. He roared! The anxiety in his normally calm voice wrenched Sam free and she ran toward him.

The fallen animal was Flo, a **manatee**. Her calves were wailing and the reason was clear.

Their mother was floating, belly up, on the surface of their pool. Her two-ton bulk turned once to reveal thick folds of dark grey skin and deep wrinkles. She looked like a giant slug, a cross between a walrus and whale. Her snout was big and round. Sam had never seen anything like her. Flo's soft underside rolled back and forth as her babies frantically swam in circles around her lifeless body. She's dead! Sam panicked. But Flo's soft whiskers fluttered from the barest hint of breath.

"Get in," Jacob ordered, his self-control now completely lost. But Sam backed slowly away.

"She's dead. What do you want me to do?"

"Get in. Get in. Get in." Jacob's voice had risen to a new octave.

"Sam, you have to try." It was Francis's voice. He was there, in the pool with the manatees. He had found a way through the underwater passages, and he was there to help.

That was all Sam had to see. Whether it was shame or grace that forced Sam into the water, she would never know. But in she went and waded carefully toward Flo. Sam touched her body. It was still warm. Then she stroked her belly, her throat. Softly at first, then more urgently, her hands working harder. The infants were still wailing. Francis spoke to them in words Sam couldn't understand, and their cries stopped.

"Sing," Jacob said.

Words came to Sam's lips as if another were speaking for her. She let them come, singing the verse of her dreams, the song of the orca.

"I am the sea . . . " Sam whispered.

"Louder."

"I am the sea," Sam sang. "Don't cry for me. Don't look for me there, I am everywhere."

Sam sang over and over again, stronger each time. As she held tight to Flo, and looked at the hope on Francis's face, she forgot her own fears. She sang with a voice she had never known before.

Then Flo shuddered, convulsed, and opened her eyes. They were glazed. Sam kept singing. Slowly, painfully slowly, Flo came back to life. She rolled her huge weight around and gasped for air.

"My babies," were the first words out of Flo's mouth.

"They're okay," said Sam. She began to laugh with relief. She laughed until she ached. Flo merely tilted her head and looked at Sam as if she had gone mad. Her calves crowded close to their mother, nuzzling and cooing softly. It was a picture of such love, such simple love, Sam was visibly stirred. Then Flo reached out with her fat stubby nose and kissed both Sam and Francis on the cheek. Francis wiggled his body with affection.

The five of them—Flo, her babies, Sam, and Francis—hung in the water as sunken clouds, lost in their joy.

Sam could have stayed there forever, she thought, but knew she had to leave this happy scene and set to work. Urgently. She had to make sure the other animals had survived the blast. Sam followed Dapper and Jacob through the cave as they counted the creatures, searching for any who were hurt or missing.

In the middle of the room they found a pile of stone in a little pool. They heard a faint whistle and Sam scrambled into the shallow water and began pushing the smaller rocks away. They were heavy and she grew tired but still she pressed on. She heaved and grunted under the strain and soon only two rocks remained, submerged beneath the surface. She reached for the largest, but when she grabbed it by the sides, it moved. Sam started.

First one scaly leg appeared, then another, a third, a fourth. Dapper laughed out loud. "Come out, come out, whoever you are," he sang. But the sea turtle refused to show its head. "Come on, Petulia," Dapper urged. Slowly, timidly, a green nose poked out, then the eyes, and soon Petulia's whole head was bouncing about in the water. She peered around a bit to get her bearings, then she ducked back into her house. Her shell had saved her.

Sam, Jacob, and Dapper searched through the rest of the pools. Everyone else seemed to be okay. Except, except . . .

"The seals!" Sam shouted. "Where are the seals?"

She ran to the place where their special room had been but the entrance was blocked with a pile of rock. She grabbed at the boulders, but they would not budge. As she'd given up hope, helplessness closing in, the chatter of a hundred alarmed voices spilled out behind her. Sam turned to find the whole colony of seals bobbing in what used to be Nicky's pool. Sam remembered all the pools had passageways and knew the seals had found their way through. What a reunion!

When Sam finally sat down to rest, she asked, "What is going on?"

"I don't know, exactly. Those boats Francis saw must be doing this," said Jacob.

"What happened to Flo? Why did she pass out like that?"

"Shock. From the sound of the propellers. Flo was cut by the blades of a propeller on a motor boat. People were racing it near her home off the Florida coast. She thought the sounds it made were calls of distress, and she went toward the boat to help."

Jacob stopped and looked very closely at Sam. Sam knew she was being studied by that big old fish in his filmy, fluid bubble. "Tell me, Jacob. I want to know the rest."

"The people in the boat saw Flo. They tied a rope around her and dragged her along behind as they sped through the water. When she grew tired, they turned and ran her down. She will always remember that. Her cut has healed but she has another wound so deep I doubt she'll ever be able to leave here."

Sam had arrived in this place off a boat. Did Jacob think her boat was bad? "My uncle says sailboats have small propellers, but they're hidden behind the keel," she said. " I don't think they can hurt animals."

"I believe you are right," said Jacob.

Sam was very, very glad to hear that. Still, it had been people, her kind, that had done this awful thing to that gentle giant.

"I wish I wasn't human," Sam said then, angry at herself and ashamed. "What about her babies? Will they be all right?"

"Flo knows she must let them go some day. They would have no kind of life down here."

"But," Sam stammered, "but they could get killed out there."

"She understands that. But we all have to go. Most of us do, some day. This isn't the real world, this place. We have to do the things we were born to do. We have to search for food, swim, breed, teach. Or we die."

"But *you're* here. *You're* okay."

A spiral of light spun through Jacob's bubble, lifting him to the ceiling.

Jacob spoke from high above, and his words rolled down on Sam like cushioned boulders, stronger, deeper, heavy with age and agelessness.

"I am not really here, Sam," he said. "I am the spirit of the sea. My body died years ago. But you can save the rest of me."

Then Jacob opened his mouth and a large, ivory-colored pearl fell into Sam's hand. She closed her fist around it, squeezing it as if it would release all the secrets of the universe. Pearls are beauty made from pain. It was a perfect gift.

"I must go," Sam said.

"Yes, you are ready now." It was Jacob's voice from somewhere beyond the walls, beyond the waves. Sam knew she would never see him again. Sam knew she would likely never see many of these creatures again. But she was not afraid, nor was she lonely. They all shared the same world, and Sam was part of it. She looked around the room, and all eyes seemed to be on her. No one spoke. The love for these animals rose in Sam like a big balloon. She knew what she had to do.

She put on her life vest then lowered herself into the pool where the little sea lion pup had died. Sadness clouded her heart, but she let it go. She called for Francis and his brother and sister. They dove beneath their pool and re-emerged in hers. She called for Dapper, and he flew into her arms. She looked at her friends, held them as close as she could, then closed her eyes. Sam began to chant: "I am the sea. Don't cry for me. Don't look for me there. I am everywhere. I am the sea . . ."

A low rumble began to creep through the cave. It climbed through the waters and echoed off the ocean floor. Like a runaway train it overtook Sam, the dolphins, and Dapper. They were swallowed by a rush of air, then hurled through funnels of water. Sam was hurtling, then floating, then nothing.

CHAPTER ELEVEN

THE VICTORY OF LOVE

"I THINK SHE'S coming to." Aunt Margaret's voice sounded like it came from the end of a long tunnel.

"I am the sea," Sam mumbled. "I am the sea..."

"Sam, Sam." Uncle Dan shook her. "Sam, wake up."

Light, bright light, punctured Sam's foggy dream. She opened her eyes and gazed into the grinning faces of her aunt and uncle and a uniformed man. They all hovered over her as if she were a precious diamond on display.

Her aunt was crying, and so was her uncle.

"We picked you up a few hours ago, floating on the surface close to where you fell overboard. I don't know why, but we searched for three days and couldn't find you anywhere. Then..." Her aunt's voice broke. Sam was dazed but otherwise all right.

The bump on her head had all but healed. She smelled of stale sea water and salt and wrinkled her nose. They had wrapped her in several thick blankets, and she felt hot.

"We were afraid that you had **hypothermia**, that the cold water had made you sick. You were in the water so long," Uncle Dan explained.

Their faces looked different. The boat looked different. Sam blinked as if to clear the image. It seemed as if, somehow, everything was both familiar yet new. Whatever it was, it was real. And Sam breathed deeply of the fresh air and the scents of human closeness. She struggled to free herself of the blankets. "I must get up."

"But, Sam, you should rest," Aunt Margaret cautioned, placing a plump, warm hand on Sam's shoulder. "You've just been through a terrible ordeal."

Yes, I have, Sam thought, and probed the corners of her mind for memories. Why couldn't she remember?

"Who's that?" Sam asked, pointing to the uniformed man by the door.

"He's an officer in the Coast Guard. They came when we sent our distress call, and they've been helping us ever since."

"Thank you," Sam said, remembering her manners. The officer told Aunt Margaret he would leave for his boat but would wait there until they were absolutely certain Sam had fully recovered.

"We appreciate it," Uncle Dan told him, grinning broadly from ear to ear, his smile as big as his heart.

"Wait," Sam called. There was something she had to do, but she couldn't quite remember what.

"What is it?" Aunt Margaret asked.

"I, I don't know," Sam said, frustrated and bewildered.

"It's okay, dear. You tell us when you're ready."

The Coast Guard officer winked at Sam. "I'm glad we found you, little lady. You had us quite worried. We looked for you a long time." Uncle Dan followed the officer up the stairs and onto the deck.

Sam got up, slowly, much to her aunt's dismay, and followed her uncle outside. She peered across the vast waters, now a deep blue and barely lapping their boat in the light breeze. The last time she had seen this sea, there was no horizon, hidden as it was in grey clouds and swirling rains. The ocean had been a terrifying force then. Now it was as gentle as a deer, cradling the boat and caressing its hull with sweet whispers of sound. But something was wrong in this calm scene. Something not so innocent. Sam looked right, then left. A huge vessel was blotting the seascape about half a mile from where she stood. Its black hull sat like a quiet hunter, waiting to strike. Sam grew tense. Why did this sight alarm her? She had seen many ships like it, coming and going through Boston Harbor. What was it?

Sam's insides screamed for the truth. She wished she could remember and she yelled at the wind, "What? What?" Her call was answered by the chattering of three dolphins who were engaged in a sporting caper of tag near the sailboat's stern. Sam watched, enchanted. She had seen these playful creatures before, earlier in their journey, but when she looked closer, it seemed their game was not a game at all. The largest of the three was pointing his beak at Sam, then at the black ship. He ducked into the water, circled, and pointed again. What was he doing? What was he trying to say?

Sam thrust her hands into the pockets of her jacket and toyed with a small, smooth rock lying on the seam. Absently, she took the rock out of her pocket and rolled in between her fingers and palm. She looked down. It wasn't a rock at all. It was the most beautiful pearl she had ever seen. And in its core were all the mysteries of the last few days. Sam looked at the dolphins and cried out loud. Francis! Bonnie! Dorey!

The joy, the fear, the amazement, the pain of everything she had seen— been a part of—flooded through her mind and filled her spirit.

"Aunt Margaret, Uncle Dan!" she called, barely able to get the words out as her thoughts raced ahead. "What is that ship?"

"It's a research drilling ship. It tests for oil and mineral deposits. They've been blasting dynamite. The sound waves from the explosions bounce off the ocean floor to tell them how far down it is. Then they take a pipe with a drill inside and bore holes in the floor to get samples of the rock. They've been working here for the last couple of days."

The thuds must have been the explosions. And the drilling! It was all threatening the world below. "You mustn't let them," Sam stated flatly, catching her aunt and uncle off guard.

"What do you mean?" Margaret asked.

"I mean, you can't let them test here. You can't."

"I don't like it any more than you do, Sam. But we need oil to run our cars, our boats, the factories that make the things we use. We need minerals for fuel and other uses. We're the ones who create the demand, not them." Uncle Dan pointed to the big ship. "Don't be mad at them."

Sam was confused. They were right. It didn't make sense. Sam had ridden in cars and insisted her parents buy her factory-made things she didn't need.

"But aren't there other ways to make those things run?"

"Sure," Uncle Dan said. "Research has been done. But," he shrugged, "oil still seems to be the cheapest way. And as long as there's oil we can get to easily, well . . ."

"What if they couldn't get to it easily? What if they were going to destroy a lot of life down there? Doesn't that count?"

"It should," her uncle said.

"Well," Sam took a deep breath, "they would be. There's a whole world down there. A special place where sick and frightened animals go to heal. They've all been hurt by people and what we do."

Margaret and Dan glanced at each other and tried to hide the smiles forming on their lips. "Sam, you were lost at sea for three days," Aunt Margaret said softly. "You were unconscious when we found you. The mind does funny things to you when you're hurt."

"No," said Sam, frustrated. All adults were the same. All they saw was what was directly in front of them. How was she going to convince them? Her aunt reached for her then, but Sam stepped away and headed for the bow.

There was nowhere to go, nothing she could do. That's not true, a little voice said, somewhere from a place beyond Sam's dreams. One person *can* do a lot. She walked carefully back to the adults, searching for the right words.

"You've got to believe me," Sam began, but her words were cut short by a sound exploding far below the surface. A large steel crane on the deck of the big ship was lowering pipes, all connected to each other, into the water. It was the drilling rig gearing up for a push through the sea floor, through the cave with all Sam's new friends sitting like unknowing targets in its path. The three dolphins swirled in a frenzy, crying out at the intrusion.

"Please," Sam begged, "please believe me." A series of thuds jolted through the water.

Sam's eyes pored over the ocean in search of Francis and his siblings. Francis had disappeared. Sam knew he had gone to help the others in the World Beyond the Waves. More sonic booms ripped through the depths. Dorey was calling desperately for his brother, then he dove deep, the water swallowing his trail. Moments later, Dorey shot through the surface and screeched at the sailboat. Bonnie circled around and around, lost in panic.

Sam never stopped to think. She jumped feet first off the boat, then swam frantically toward the big ship. The salt water stung her eyes, but Sam swam on, lungs bursting. She had to find Francis.

Just as she had given up hope, she spotted a grey form hanging in the ocean like a sack of flesh. His tail fluttered, the last sign of his struggle to get to back to his brother and sister. Sam burst through the surface and cried, "It's Francis. He's hurt. Uncle Dan, Uncle Dan!"

Both the Coast Guard's and Uncle Dan's vessels were moving toward Sam. Dan's sailboat drew beside her first and she was pulled onto the deck by a very worried uncle. His scolding would wait, however, as all eyes were on the action in front of them.

The Coast Guard lowered a big net into the water and pulled Francis inside. Sam knew how much nets frightened Francis and she bit down on her lip in sympathy. Dan threw his dinghy over the side of his boat, jumped in, and paddled furiously toward the injured animal.

Dan was a marine biologist and knew about things like this. Sam watched from the deck as her uncle examined the dolphin, prodding and stroking. Sam couldn't stand it. She tried to pull herself free of her aunt's arms, but Margaret held fast.

"No you don't," she said. "Your uncle knows what to do."

Minutes, too many minutes later, Uncle Dan paddled back. The expression on his face said everything.

"Nooooooo . . . " Sam wailed. The net lowered Francis back into the sea and Sam watched as her friend—her dear, beloved, courageous friend—left her forever. He'd been hit by an explosion in his desperate attempt to protect the world below.

Dorey and Bonnie circled over the place where Francis had gone down. Their cries were the cries of the ages. Their eyes, confused and filled with loss, broke Sam's heart. Her grief turned to anger. Furious, unleashed anger.

"You have to stop that boat," she screamed. "There are more animals down there, many more. They live in a secret place. Make them stop!" Uncle Dan and Aunt Margaret, usually quiet, gentle people who had worked all their lives to understand and protect the sea, needed no more convincing. For their love of that great, undiscovered world and for their love of Sam, they bolted into action.

Dan called the Coast Guard and informed them he had strong reason to believe there were large numbers of protected species in these waters. Protected, he said, by law. Then he did what Sam would never forget and never be able to thank him for. That quiet, gentle man who never, ever raised his voice, closed his eyes, sucked in his breath, and yelled. He yelled into the radio with everything he had: "That ship must be ordered to stop!" Several radio transmissions later, Sam and Dan and Margaret were told the ship would be pulling away. The drilling crew did not want to risk further danger to the animals.

Sam watched the dark fortress weigh anchor and cut through the waves. Relief washed over her. It was gone and, if fortune was with them, it would not be back.

Sam, Dan and Margaret walked hand in hand out to the deck. Bonnie and Dorey had left, but Sam knew Francis had taught them well. His life had been for them, she thought, and his death had been for Flo and Sito and all the creatures of that undersea world, those now there and those to follow. A great tear of sorrow fell down Sam's cheek. "I love you, Francis," Sam whispered.

The three turned to watch the sky settle into pink and bronze as the sun began its graceful descent into the night. All was quiet, with each person absorbed in his or her own thoughts. Uncle Dan brushed a strand of hair from Sam's face.

"Are you ready to tell us what really happened to you, Sam?" he asked. The answer to his question came, as so many answers do, from the sea itself.

Out of the depths a sound emerged, low and quiet at first, but building and climbing. A deep and strange chorus rose and grew. It lifted the waves and filled the sea itself. The haunting chords swam around the boat, as if the world had opened up and begun to sing. The sound took shape and in one final whirl of music, Sam heard the unmistakable words of "thank you." She knew the World Beyond the Waves had been saved.

A tropic bird flew on the orchestra of wind and landed on the railing beside Sam. "Dapper," Sam said, overjoyed. "You came back with me." But the funny little bird merely squawked and ruffled his feathers. Sam looked hurt. "Oh no, you can't talk to me anymore," she said. The bird paid her no heed.

"You can talk to us," Dan said then. "You've come home." Sam fell into her aunt and uncle's arms and knew at last she *had* come home. She would never take it for granted again. She would think about all the things she bought and used and threw away. And she knew she could never be as thoughtless as she had once been. For she had friends who depended on her now. Who depend on all of us.

Sam looked at the tropic bird and was saddened to know the magic of that place beyond the waves was magic she had shared for those few short days and those days only. But she remembered then what Dapper had told her right after she had arrived.

"I think, rather," he had said, "you can understand." *That* was the answer. Sam held the special pearl in her hand and knew it would always be with her.

"Thank you Dapper, my little friend," she said to the tropic bird. As he spread his wings for flight, he turned his mischievous eyes toward her. And Sam saw it clearly—he winked.

GLOSSARY

Atlantic Sturgeon: (page 65) The Atlantic sturgeon is a primitive fish which lives in both fresh and salt water. It spawns in rivers. Many sturgeon are caught for their meat but the female's eggs also are sold as very expensive caviar. These eggs are removed from the female before they are laid, resulting in the death of that female.

Blue Marlin: (page 65) The blue marlin is a fish often pursued by sport fishermen because of its powerful ability to fight the line once it is hooked, and for its great beauty. Once defeated, it is often stuffed and mounted as a trophy for the wall. It can grow to a length of 12 feet (4 meters) and a weight of 175 pounds (80 kg). It is found in the Atlantic Ocean from Florida and the West Indies to the tip of Long Island.

Bottlenose Dolphin: (page 17) The bottlenose dolphin ranges in length from 9 to 12 feet (3 to 4 meters) and in weight from 500 to 1400 pounds (220 to 640 kg). It is a highly intelligent sea mammal. Dolphins are very social creatures and usually travel in small groups of about a dozen individuals or larger packs of several hundred. They form strong family attachments and live in temperate ocean waters around the world.

Coelacanth: (page 30) The coelacanth (seal-a-kanth) is a large, deep-water fish once thought to be extinct. Fossils indicate it dates back many millions of years, but the first discovery of an actual specimen was made in 1938. Others were found later off the Comoro Islands. None of these specimens lived through capture, as it appears the coelacanth cannot survive a move to shallower water.

Dorsal Fin: (page 46) Dorsal fins are located along the centerline of the back, on fish and sea mammals. Dorsal fins may stand alone, or there may be several lined up in a row. They may be fleshy or bony. Marine biologists often use the distinctive shape and size of the dorsal fin to identify each individual in a species. In this way, the fins are somewhat like fingerprints.

Drift Net: (page 44) Drift or gill nets are made of mesh large enough for just the fish head to pass through, snagging the fish at its gills. Drift nets are used to catch salmon, tuna, cod, and other kinds of fish. Since the 1980s, the use of huge drift nets, assembled together into miles of netting, has created problems of overfishing and has caused the accidental death of thousands of other species such as dolphins, sharks, turtles, and whales.

Drift Net Fishing: (page 44) Drift net fishing is a highly controversial, morally questionable method of fishing. Larger drift net boats may lay up to 30 miles (50 km) of net each day. A single net can rake in hundreds of species of sea life, damaging that entire area's ecosystem. Drift nets have been referred to as "walls of death."

Ecosystem: An ecosystem is the interaction of living beings: how they cycle and pass on nutrients and energy, how they control their populations. In ecosystems, all energy comes originally from the sun. A small part of this energy is captured by plants, then part of this is passed on to herbivores (plant-eating animals), then to carnivores (flesh-eating animals). The earth is one giant ecosystem comprised of many smaller ecosystems, each almost self-contained. Each ecosystem has a "food chain" which begins with the smallest organisms and ends, usually, with the larger carnivores. If any part of the ecosystem is damaged or destroyed, it affects all other parts, because each part is "food" for another living being further up the chain.

Grouper: (page 46) Groupers are predatory fish found in tropical or temperate seas around the world. They have smaller bodies and large mouths, and they come in a variety of colors. They range in size from one to 140 inches (2.5 to 360 cm).

Hypothermia: (page 77) This is the lowering of body temperature to dangerous levels caused by extended exposure to cold. Heart rate slows and mental functions become impaired. In the worst cases, coma and death can result. People trapped in cold water for even a few minutes are at risk of hypothermia. The treatment involves slowly raising body temperature to normal.

Manatee: (page 70) The manatee is a large sea mammal. The Florida manatee lives off that state's east and west coasts. It is highly endangered and it is believed only about 1,800 remain. Many are badly injured or killed each year by the blades of motorboats, fishing lines and crab traps. Manatees are extremely large but gentle creatures. They may reach a length of more than 12 feet (4 meters) and a weight of more than 2,700 pounds (1200 kg).

MARPOL: Stands for Marine Pollution Treaty of 1973. In 1987, the United States ratified an amendment to MARPOL which prohibited the ocean dumping of plastic materials. The most common visible type of human-made garbage in the sea is plastic. Plastic takes a very long time to break down and it accumulates as we dump more and more of it every day. In a single year, over a one 300-mile (500 km) stretch of Texas coastline, almost 16,000 six-pack rings were discovered. If you use six packs, cut the rings before you throw them away. Thousands of sea mammals die every year from getting entangled in plastic debris. Eighty of the 280 species of sea birds eat plastic, much of which may cause internal damage. Plastic clings to coral reefs, causing damage and death.

Orca: (page 58) Orca are also known as killer whales. They form strong family bonds and are the greatest predators of the ocean. They seem to hunt in organized packs and circle their prey, closing in for the kill. Their aggressive behavior becomes reversed with humans, as they appear to accept us as their equals. Males reach an average of 25 feet (7.6 meters); females, 21 feet (6.4 meters). They appear to favor the colder waters of both northern and southern hemispheres, but they are widely dispersed around the world. They may travel thousands of miles each year.

Petrels: (page 30) Petrels are oceanic birds that range over wide areas. They spend most of their lives at sea and only venture toward land to breed. They are found mostly in the southern hemisphere but some live in the northern areas. They are strong flyers and have long wings. They range in color from black to gray or brown, with white patches. They lay a single egg which both the male and female care for. Storm petrels were given this name by sailors who believed the presence of these birds warned of an approaching storm. They are from five to ten inches (14 to 25 cm) in length.

Rays and Skates: (page 66) Rays and skates are very flat fish that live on the bottom in shallower water. The sting ray has a poison gland at the base of the spine on its tail. It can inflict a painful wound.

Silky Shark: (page 45) The silky shark grows to about 9 feet (3 meters) in length and 220 to 330 pounds (100 to 150 kg) in weight. In comparison to other sharks, it is smooth to the touch. It feeds upon groupers and snappers on the ocean bottom. It is frequently caught in drift nets.

Snapper: (page 46) There are actually about 230 species of marine food fish called snappers. They have large jaws, sharp teeth, and a downward sloping snout. Most live near the shoreline, but some are found in the middle of the ocean and at great depths. They usually travel in small groups but sometimes can unite with other groups to form schools of millions. They are mostly nocturnal (active at night), and sometimes color-blind. They range up to 3 feet (1meter) in length.

Stalactite and Stalagmite: (page 37) These are formations of calcium carbonate found on the ceiling ('c' for ceiling and for stala'c'tite), and on the ground ('g' for ground and for stala'g'mite) of caves. Water that seeps into a cave carries carbon dioxide which unites with the limestone of the cave rock to form crystals. When the crystals pile up, they form stalactites, which look like icicles hanging from the ceiling, and stalagmites, which look like pillars or big teeth jutting up from the floor.

Tropic Bird: (page 18) The tropic bird grows to about 30 inches (75 cm) in length, but its long tail feathers and slender wings make it appear much larger. It roams over great distances along the tropical latitudes of the world's oceans. It has a graceful, wheeling flight and floats easily on water, although it is quite awkward on land. It feeds on small fish and squid, which it catches by diving. It is widely considered one of the most beautiful of all sea birds.

THE TEAM

KATE KEMPTON is an environmental educator who has developed workshops, games, books and other material designed to teach children and adults the real issues surrounding the environment. Ms. Kempton earned a Master of Arts degree in Journalism from the University of Western Ontario in Canada. She has worked on special assignment as a news writer and segment producer at CTV Television, co-writing Canada A.M. Kate is married and resides in Toronto, Canada.

CAROL TREHEARN is a native of Cape Town, South Africa. Having lived most of her life in Johannesburg, Ms. Trehearn has obtained degrees from both Damelin College and Rosebank College. She delivers yachts throughout the world. It was while delivering a yacht that she developed the idea for this story. Today, Carol continues traveling.

LARRY SALK has been a freelance illustrator for over thirty years and has specialized in portraiture, a specialty that has led him from motion picture and television posters to sports celebrity memorabilia. This is his second children's book.